Discovery

Exploring Places
大探險家

Gina D. B. Clemen

Editor: Daniela Penzavalle
Design and art direction: Nadia Maestri
Computer graphics: Maura Santini
Picture research: Laura Lagomarsino

©2010 BLACK CAT
a brand of DE AGOSTINI SCUOLA spa, Novara
©2013 THE COMMERCIAL PRESS (H.K.) LTD., Hong Kong

Picture credits
Cideb Archive; De Agostini Picture Library: 6, 8 bottom, 13 top, 15, 25 bottom, 27
bottom, 36, 37, 38, 39, 54, 55, 56 top, 67, 83 top, 84, 87 bottom; © MAPS.com / Corbis:
8 top; The Bridgeman Art Library / Getty Images: 13 bottom; © Blue Lantern Studio
/ Corbis: 14; © MARKA / Alamy: 16; © Robert Harding World Imagery / Corbis: 17;
Library of Congress / Science Photo Library / Contrasto: 18; National Geographic /
Getty Images: 19; National Maritime Museum, London: 25 top; SuperStock / Getty
Images: 27 top; Andrew Geiger / Getty Images: 43; © Bettmann / CORBIS: 45, 85;
Hulton Archive / Getty Images: 48, 66, 70; Peeter Viisimaa / Getty Images: 52; TRI
STAR PICTURES/ Album: 53; © Frans Lanting / Corbis: 56 bottom; Time & Life
Pictures / Getty Images: 57, 58, 64; Popperfoto / Getty Images: 65; © PoodlesRock /
Corbis: 68; Travel Ink /Getty Images: 69; BRYNA PRODUCTION / UNITED ARTISTS
/ Album: 75; Webphoto: 77; WALT DISNEY PRODUCTIONS / Album: 78 top; 20TH
CENTURY FOX / Album: 78 bottom; PARAMOUNT TV / Album: 79; UNITED
INTERNATIONAL PICTURES / Album: 80; © Liam Davis / Corbis: 83 bottom;
PLANETARY VISIONS LTD / SCIENCE PHOTO LIBRARY / Contrasto: 86; Getty
Images: 88.

書　　名：*Exploring Places* 大探險家
作　　者：Gina D. B. Clemen
責任編輯：黃家麗　　王朴真
封面設計：張　　毅　李小丹
出　　版：商務印書館 (香港) 有限公司
　　　　　香港筲箕灣耀興道 3 號東滙廣場 8 樓
　　　　　http://www.commercialpress.com.hk
發　　行：香港聯合書刊物流有限公司
　　　　　香港新界大埔汀麗路 36 號中華商務印刷大廈 3 字樓
印　　刷：中華商務彩色印刷有限公司
　　　　　香港新界大埔汀麗路 36 號中華商務印刷大廈 14 字樓
版　　次：2013 年 4 月第 1 版第 1 次印刷
　　　　　© 2013 商務印書館 (香港) 有限公司
　　　　　ISBN 978 962 07 1997 4
　　　　　Printed in Hong Kong

版權所有　不得翻印

Contents

The text is recorded in full.

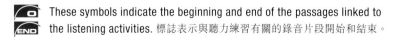

These symbols indicate the beginning and end of the passages linked to
the listening activities. 標誌表示與聽力練習有關的錄音片段開始和結束。

Before you read

1 Vocabulary

Match the pictures (A-D) with their correct names (1-4). You can use a dictionary to help you.

1   Viking longship   3   Greek ship
2   Egyptian cedar wood   4   Egyptian papyrus reeds

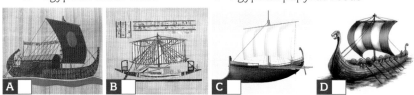

A ☐   B ☐   C ☐   D ☐

 2 Listening

PET

Listen to the first part of Chapter One and choose the correct answer — A, B or C.

1   The first inhabitants of Africa

   A ☐   did not travel.
   B ☐   went to other continents.
   C ☐   left some written records.

2   The Egyptians were the first explorers

   A ☐   to travel in boats.
   B ☐   to travel to India.
   C ☐   who left records of their trips.

3   Egyptian ships were made of

   A ☐   cedar wood.
   B ☐   papyrus reeds.
   C ☐   tin.

4   The city of Carthage was founded by

   A ☐   the Phoenicians.
   B ☐   the Greeks.
   C ☐   the Egyptians.

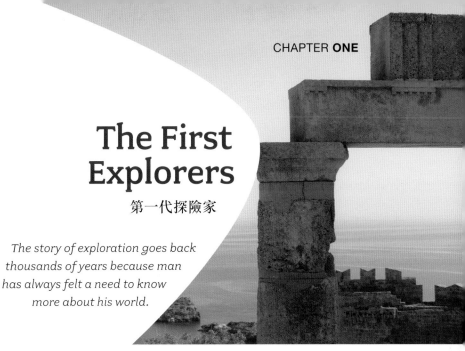

CHAPTER ONE

The First Explorers

第一代探險家

The story of exploration goes back thousands of years because man has always felt a need to know more about his world.

The story of exploration goes back many thousands of years. Scientists tell us that the first human beings lived in Africa and then slowly moved to other areas which are the present-day Middle East, Europe, Asia and North and South America. They were the first explorers, but we know almost nothing about them and their journeys. They left no written records or maps, and we don't know anything about the boats they sailed on during their journeys.

The first explorers who left records of their journeys were the Egyptians. From about 3900 BCE, the ancient Egyptians built boats from papyrus reeds which they tied together. They used these simple boats to carry people and goods along the River Nile.

Later the Egyptians built long wooden ships and were able to travel longer distances. Their first sea voyage was made in 2600 BCE when they sailed to Byblos in Phoenicia to buy cedar wood for building ships. They also sailed to Crete, Greece and down the Red Sea to the east coast of Africa to trade goods.

The greatest explorers of ancient times were probably the Phoenicians. They came from an area that is now Lebanon. They were excellent shipbuilders and they became the richest merchants in the Mediterranean. By 1000 BCE they were trading with Cyprus, Spain and North Africa. They founded trading centres around the Mediterranean like Carthage in North Africa, which became a rich and important city.

The ancient Greeks sent ships to explore the coasts around the Mediterranean and the Black Sea and founded colonies [1].

---

1. **colonies**：殖民地

Egyptian wooden boat from the tomb of Sennefer, 18th dynasty (about 1567-1320 BC), Valley of the Nobles, Thebes.

In the third century BCE a Greek scientist and explorer called Pytheas made a famous voyage into the North Atlantic. He sailed from the Greek colony of Massalia (present-day Marseilles) in southern France to south-west Britain to look for tin [1], which he found in Cornwall.

Alexander the Great of Macedon (356-323 BCE) was a great Greek military leader. Although Alexander the Great was not an explorer, he and his army travelled to and conquered [2] many lands and founded seventy cities, among which Alexandria in Egypt. When he died at the age of 32, he was the ruler of the largest empire in the western world and a legend [3] in his own time. He ruled most of the lands between Greece and India.

1. **tin** : 錫
2. **conquered** : 征服
3. **legend** : 傳奇人物

Greek boat, mosaic tiles, Tunis.

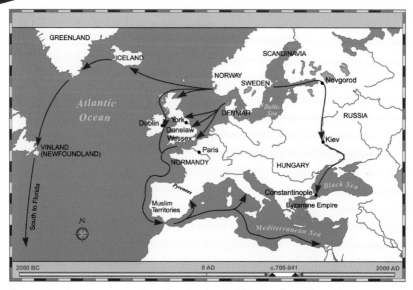

A map showing the routes of exploration by the Vikings throughout Europe and towards the New World.

About a thousand years later, the Vikings, whose home was in Scandinavia, were great explorers and navigators. Their ships were about 30 metres long and were called longships; they could carry up to 80 men. Between the late 700s and 1100 CE they sailed to western Europe, Russia, Iceland, Greenland and North America. In western Europe they attacked villages and founded colonies in Normandy, France; Sicily, Italy; Dublin, Ireland and York, England.

A Viking longship.

The Vikings also travelled to present-day Greece and Turkey. Some of them joined the Guard of the Emperor of Byzantium in Constantinople which is now Istanbul in Turkey.

The text and **beyond**

PET ① Comprehension check

For each question choose the correct answer — A, B, C or D.

1   The ancient Egyptians

   A ☐   did not leave records of their journeys.
   B ☐   slowly moved to the Middle East.
   C ☐   sailed on papyrus reed boats on the River Nile.
   D ☐   travelled on foot along the River Nile to the east coast of Africa.

2   The Egyptians sailed to Phoenicia

   A ☐   to buy cedar wood.
   B ☐   in papyrus reed boats.
   C ☐   to buy wooden ships.
   D ☐   which was on the coast of Africa.

3   The richest merchants of the Mediterranean were

   A ☐   the Greeks.
   B ☐   the Egyptians.
   C ☐   the Phoenicians.
   D ☐   the Vikings.

4   Pytheas sailed to Cornwall

   A ☐   to fight a war.
   B ☐   to found a Greek colony.
   C ☐   to visit Massalia.
   D ☐   to buy tin.

5   The Vikings travelled long distances

   A ☐   because they had good maps.
   B ☐   and founded colonies in North America.
   C ☐   and went to live in Turkey.
   D ☐   in their longships.

2 Vocabulary

Circle the word that doesn't belong and explain why.

1 gold   tin   wood   steel
2 record   map   diary   letter
3 state   village   town   city
4 ruler   merchant   queen   king
5 Greece   Greenland   Egyptian   Turkey

3 Vocabulary

A **Find the six names of the first important explorers in the word square and circle them.**

P	B	D	V	Y	T	L	U	M	B	V	I	K	E
A	H	I	B	A	L	E	X	A	N	D	E	R	N
W	U	O	G	T	A	C	R	E	S	T	D	B	G
O	P	S	E	G	Y	P	T	I	A	N	S	E	S
S	Y	F	M	N	O	U	K	J	B	P	C	R	D
V	T	J	C	Y	I	S	A	G	R	E	E	K	S
B	H	P	N	J	F	C	H	E	X	I	K	S	X
G	E	R	D	W	S	V	I	K	I	N	G	S	M
O	A	G	R	E	A	Y	N	A	E	V	O	G	L
D	S	O	S	M	R	E	K	L	N	Z	U	X	E
Z	H	F	P	Y	O	N	R	M	P	S	O	N	F

B **Write a sentence using each name.**

Before you read

1 Vocabulary

Match the pictures (A-D) with the words (1-4). Use a dictionary to help you.

1   spices   3   navigation instruments
2   astrolabe   4   passage

A ☐   B ☐   C ☐   D ☐

2 Listening

Listen to the first part of Chapter Two and choose the correct answer, — A, B or C.

1   Aristotle and Ptolemy

    A ☐   believed the Earth was flat.
    B ☐   lived in the Indies.
    C ☐   did not believe the Earth was flat.

2   Christopher Columbus wanted to

    A ☐   find a sea-route to the Indies.
    B ☐   explore America.
    C ☐   cross the Pacific Ocean.

3   Which country financed Columbus's voyage?

    A ☐   Portugal
    B ☐   Spain
    C ☐   Italy

4   Where did Columbus land on 12 October 1492?

    A ☐   America
    B ☐   Spice Islands
    C ☐   Bahamas

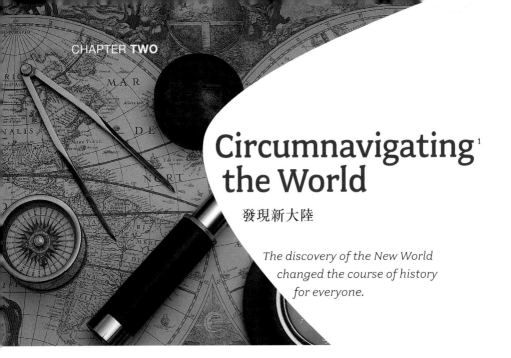

CHAPTER TWO

Circumnavigating[1] the World

發現新大陸

The discovery of the New World
changed the course of history
for everyone.

For centuries people thought that the Earth was flat. But the Greek philosopher Aristotle and the Egyptian astronomer Ptolemy believed the earth was round. By the late 15th century many scholars[2] agreed with them. But how could they prove this idea?

An idea that changed the world

The first person who proved that the world was round was an Italian navigator from Genoa called Cristoforo Colombo. In Spain he was known as Cristobal Colon and to the rest of the world, Christopher Columbus. He believed he could find a sea-route to islands that Europeans called the Spice Islands, which are the present-day Moluccas. At that time spices were very important because they stopped meat and other foods from going bad. And

1. **circumnavigating** : 環航
2. **scholars** : 學者

Christopher Columbus (15th century).

if they went bad, spices helped to hide the unpleasant taste.

Columbus believed he could reach the Indies in the East by travelling towards the West, across the Atlantic Ocean. Like all explorers he was a brave man and an excellent navigator. At first nobody wanted to finance[1] his voyage, but Columbus went to talk to King Ferdinand and Queen Isabella of Spain and they agreed to help him.

1. **finance**：資助

The First Voyage, Ferdinand and Isabella seeing Christopher Columbus off from the Dock at Palos on Friday 3rd August 1492.

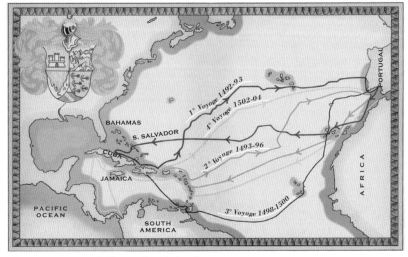

The four voyages of Christopher Columbus.

On 3 August 1492 Columbus left southern Spain and sailed West across the Atlantic Ocean with three small sailing ships. A lot of people who watched him leave thought they would never see him again, because he was sailing towards the unknown. After all, he did not have any maps and only a few navigation instruments like an astrolabe.

On 12 October 1492 Columbus and his men landed on an island in the Bahamas and called it San Salvador. Columbus thought he had reached Asia. He was wrong, but his idea was correct: by sailing West you could reach the East because the world was round. Columbus did not know that the continents of North and South America were in between.

Columbus's exciting discovery opened the doors to the New World and old maps had to be changed. What other lands and riches were in the New World? Many explorers and rulers asked themselves this question.

Two great explorers circumnavigate the world

Ferdinand Magellan and Sir Francis Drake were the two greatest navigators of the sixteenth century. Both men followed almost the same route and successfully circumnavigated the world. They were both brave, intelligent men and excellent navigators.

Magellan was born in Portugal in 1480 to a noble family. He took part in several Portuguese expeditions [1] to India and the Spice Islands by sailing around the southern tip of Africa and then East, during the first part of the sixteenth century.

Ferdinand Magellan
(16th century).

When he returned to Portugal some Portuguese sailors said there was a passage that went from the Atlantic Ocean to the Pacific Ocean, at the southern tip of South America. They probably got this information from the men who took part in the expedition led by the Spanish explorer Vasco Balboa, who discovered and explored present-day Panama and reached the Pacific Ocean from the New World. Magellan decided to find the passage and sail through it on the way to the Spice Islands. He told the King of Portugal his plan, but he was not interested in the expedition. So, like Columbus, he went to Spain and looked for someone to finance him. In Spain, Magellan met King Charles V, who agreed to finance him because the spice trade was important and profitable.

---

1. **expeditions** : 探險

On 20 September 1519, Magellan sailed from Seville, Spain with five old ships and a crew of men who did not know much about sea voyages. Only a few men like Sebastian del Cano were good navigators. After crossing the Atlantic Ocean the expedition sailed down the coast of South America with very bad weather. They looked for the passage but did not find it, and Magellan's crew was tired and disappointed. They spent the long winter months in the bay of San Julian on the coast of Patagonia and the crew became very unhappy.

On 2 April 1520 there was a mutiny [1]. The mutineers [2] took three of Magellan's five ships, but Magellan fought back. After a terrible fight, Magellan was again in command of the expedition and the mutineers were beheaded [3]. A storm destroyed one of his ships and the crew was afraid, but Magellan continued his voyage.

1. **mutiny** : 暴動
2. **mutineers** : 反賊
3. **beheaded** : 砍頭

San Julian Bay, Patagonia.

A mountain along the Strait of Magellan.

In October 1520 Magellan finally discovered a narrow passage at the southern end of South America which led to the Pacific Ocean. The voyage through the 341-mile-long (550 km) passage was very difficult and dangerous because of the strong winds and sea storms. The crew of one of the ships deserted [1] Magellan and returned to Spain. In November 1520 Magellan and his three remaining ships entered the Pacific Ocean. Magellan and his men were the first Europeans to sail on the world's largest ocean. Today the passage is called the Strait of Magellan.

Magellan thought he was near the Spice Islands, but he did not realise how big the Pacific Ocean was. The days turned into weeks and the weeks turned into months, and no land was in sight. There was little food and water left on the ships and many men died of scurvy [2] and other diseases.

1. **deserted** : 拋棄
2. **scurvy** : 壞血病

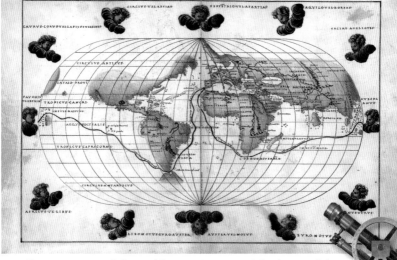

Magellan's route around the world, in a 1544 copy of the Agnese Atlas.

The crew was desperate and ate insects, old leather and mice!

At last in March 1521 Magellan's three ships reached a group of Pacific Islands which he called the Philippines, in honor of King Charles V's son, Philip. The local chief, who was friendly, gave Magellan food and drink. The chief also asked for Magellan's help in fighting a local war. Magellan and his crew agreed to help, but during the battle Magellan and eighty of his men were killed.

Only two ships, the *Vittoria* and the *Trinidad*, reached the Spice Islands, where the crew loaded a lot of spices. The *Trinidad* was in poor condition and could not sail. So only the *Vittoria*, commanded by Sebstian del Cano, sailed back to Spain, passing by the Cape of Good Hope in southern Africa. The Cape of Good Hope was discovered by the Portuguese explorer Bartolomeu Días in 1488 and he called it the Cape of Storms. King John II of Portugal later changed the name because he was happy that there was a sea route to India and the East. Of the 237 men who began the long voyage three years before, only 18 of them returned to Spain. They were the first men to sail around the world, and King Charles V and the people of Seville gave them a huge welcome.

Sir Francis Drake

Sir Francis Drake was the first Englishman to circumnavigate the world. He was born in England in 1540. Before he was thirteen he started working on a ship, and when he was twenty he became the captain of a ship when the old captain died. Drake was an experienced navigator, a great leader and a favourite of Queen Elizabeth I.

During Drake's time Spain was the most powerful nation in Europe and had many colonies in the New World. It was also an enemy of England. In 1577 Queen Elizabeth I had a secret meeting with Drake and asked him to attack the Spanish ships and colonies on the Pacific coast and bring back gold, silver and other treasure. For this reason Drake was often called a pirate.

In December 1577 he sailed from Portsmouth, in the south of England, with five ships and 166 men. He sailed across the south

Queen Elizabeth knights Sir Francis Drake on deck of the *Golden Hind*.

Atlantic, through the Strait of Magellan and attacked Spanish colonies and treasure ships on the Pacific coast. He then sailed to North America to what is now California and called it New Albion. Today there is a bay called Drake's Bay in northern California, where he stopped to repair his ships. He then crossed the Pacific and reached the Spice Islands, where he loaded his ship with spices.

During Drake's long voyage four of his ships were destroyed by storms at sea, but his ship, the *Golden Hind*, was able to return to England in September 1580 with a crew of 59 men. Queen Elizabeth was very pleased with the Spanish treasure and the spices that Drake brought back and knighted [1] him. He became a rich, important man in his country.

FACT FILE 知識檔案

The history of the Spice Islands

The native people of the Spice Islands traded spices with other Asian countries since the time of the Roman Empire (27 BCE-476 CE). Starting in the 8th century the spice trade was controlled by Muslim [2] merchants. One ancient Arabic source mentioned these islands and said that they were 'fifteen days by sea East from the island of Java'.

Between 1200 and 1500 the Italian seaport of Venice controlled the profitable spice trade in Europe. Other countries did not want to depend on Venice and wanted to find another way to get to the Spice Islands. The need to get to the Spice Islands started a lot of European exploration.

1. **knighted**：封爵
2. **Muslim**：穆斯林

The text and **beyond**

1 Comprehension check

Read these sentences about Chapter Two. Decide if each sentence is correct or incorrect. If it is correct, mark A. If it is not correct, mark B. There is an example at the beginning (0).

		A	B
0	Aristotle and Ptolemy proved that the world was round.	☐	✓
1	Columbus planned to reach the Spice Islands.	☐	☐
2	The Spanish king Charles V was interested in the spice trade and financed Magellan's voyage.	☐	☐
3	Magellan's crew was afraid and disappointed, but they obeyed him.	☐	☐
4	The Strait of Magellan was a stormy passage from the Atlantic Ocean to the Pacific Ocean.	☐	☐
5	Magellan was killed by the mutineers on his ship.	☐	☐
6	After three years, Sebastian del Cano returned to Spain with only one ship.	☐	☐
7	Sir Francis Drake became a sea captain at a young age.	☐	☐
8	Queen Elizabeth I asked Sir Francis Drake to found New Albion in North America.	☐	☐
9	Bad weather at sea destroyed all of Drake's ships except the *Golden Hind*.	☐	☐

2 Vocabulary

A Read the definitions and fill in the gaps with the correct letters.

1 people who know a lot about a certain subject _ _ _ _ _ _ _ _
2 to leave without permission _ _ _ _ _ _
3 something that brings a lot of money _ _ _ _ _ _ _ _ _ _
4 a disease caused by lack of Vitamin C _ _ _ _ _ _
5 people who are part of a mutiny _ _ _ _ _ _ _ _ _
6 to give money that is needed for a project or idea _ _ _ _ _ _ _ _
7 to sail all the way around the world _ _ _ _ _ _ _ _ _ _ _ _ _

B   Complete the sentences below with the words from part A.

1   Many men died of .... during long voyages at sea.

2   Sir Francis Drake was the first Englishman to .... the world.

3   Aristotle and Ptolemy were great ....

4   The spice trade was very ....

5   After the storm many men wanted to .... Magellan's ships.

6   Columbus asked the king and queen of Spain to .... his voyage.

7   Magellan beheaded the .... on his ships.

T: GRADE 4

3 Speaking: Food

Spices were very important in the past because they stopped food from going bad and they made it taste better. Talk about food and spices with another student. Ask and answer these questions.

1   Who does the cooking at your house?

2   What kind of food do you like?

3   What kinds of spices do you keep in your kitchen?

4   What spices do you put on your food?

5   How is food kept from going bad today?

4 Discussion

Work with another student and make a list of other important explorers during the fifteenth and sixteenth centuries. Use an encyclopedia to help you. Discuss your list with the class.

1   Who were they and what did they explore?

2   Why was the exploration important?

3   Can you find the places they explored on a map?

Before you read

1 Vocabulary

Match the pictures (A-D) with the words (1-4). Use a dictionary to help you.

1 kangaroo   **2** iceberg   **3** sea otter   **4** walrus

 A  B  C  D

2 Vocabulary

Match the words (1-4) with their meaning (A-D).

1 naturalist   **2** botanist   **3** specimen   **4** Aborigines

A ☐ A single plant or animal which is an example of a certain species.
B ☐ A person who studies animals, plants and other living things.
C ☐ A person who studies all kinds of plants.
D ☐ People who lived in Australia when the first Europeans arrived.

  3 Listening

Listen to part of Chapter Three and decide if each statement is correct or incorrect. If it is correct, put a tick (✓) in the box under A for YES. If it is not correct, put a tick in the box under B for NO.

		A	B
1	Captain Cook's first voyage to the South Pacific was a scientific expedition.	☐	☐
2	Banks and Parkinson were excellent map-makers.	☐	☐
3	The crew of the *Endeavour* ate a lot of fresh fruit.	☐	☐
4	The Dutch explored the eastern coast of Australia.	☐	☐
5	There were many new and unusual plants at Botany Bay.	☐	☐

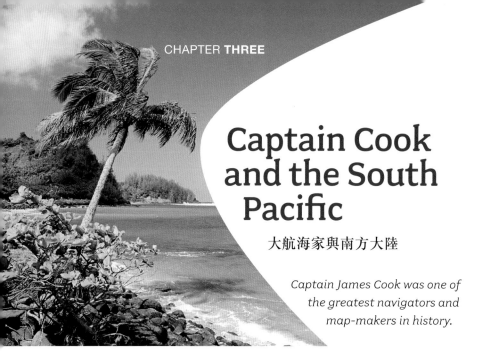

CHAPTER THREE

Captain Cook and the South Pacific

大航海家與南方大陸

Captain James Cook was one of the greatest navigators and map-makers in history.

James Cook was born in the village of Marton in the north of England in 1728. When he was a young boy he worked in a shop, but he loved the sea. When he was eighteen he started working on a ship that transported coal along the English coast, and in 1755 he decided to join the Royal Navy. This was a brave decision because life at sea was hard and dangerous.

In the 1750s Great Britain was at war with France, because both countries wanted more power and more colonies. This war was known as the Seven Years' War and it involved several European countries. In 1759 Cook joined an expedition to the St Lawrence River in Canada. The expedition conquered the French city of Quebec, and Canada became a British colony. Cook spent the next eight years making maps of the Canadian coast. He was an excellent navigator and map-maker because he knew a lot about astronomy and mathematics.

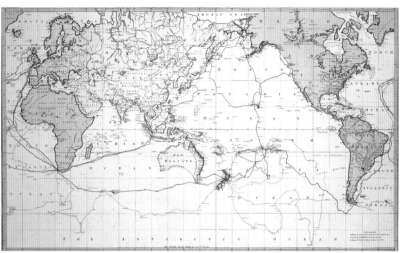

A map showing Cook's voyages to the Pacific.

The First Pacific Voyage (1768-71)

In the 18th century European rulers were interested in finding out about other parts of the world. They wanted to know how other people lived, and which plants and animals were found there. It was a time of exploration, discovery and interest in science.

In 1766 the British government asked Cook to go on a scientific expedition to the island of Tahiti in the South Pacific and observe the passage of the planet Venus across the sun. In those days information on the movement of the planets was important to navigators. He was also asked to find the Southern Continent or *Terra Australis,* an undiscovered continent which many people believed was in the world's southern oceans.

Since this was a scientific expedition there were several scientists and artists on board, like the naturalist and botanist Joseph Banks and the artist Sydney Parkinson. Their job was to find specimens and draw pictures of new plants and animals of the South Pacific.

Cook was a good captain and a responsible man, and he wanted his crew to be healthy. He knew the dangers of scurvy, so he insisted that they ate fresh fruit and vegetables. He kept the ship's medicine chest [1] well supplied with simple medicines. He also ordered that all parts of the ship should be kept very clean. Only one man died of disease during Cook's three voyages; many men died of disease during Magellan's and Drake's voyages.

Cook became the captain of the ship *Endeavour*, which left England in August 1768, sailed around Cape Horn and continued west across the Pacific. Cook and his crew arrived in Tahiti in April 1769 and started exploring the South Pacific. They sailed around New Zealand and discovered the Southern Island. Cook made a map of the complete coastline.

He then sailed west and reached the south-eastern coast of the Australian continent. Dutch explorers were the first Europeans to sail along the western coast of Australia in the 17th century, but Cook was the first European to explore the eastern coast and make excellent

1.　**medicine chest** : 藥箱

maps. He claimed both New Zealand and Australia for Great Britain [1].

In April 1770 Cook and his crew landed in Botany Bay, a name that was given to the bay by Captain Cook because of the many new plants found there. Cook and his men were attacked by two Aborigines who shot darts [2] at them, but Cook did not want to kill them; he frightened them away by shooting his gun into the air.

Captain Cook Landing at Botany Bay by Emmanuel Phillips Fox (19th century).

In Australia the naturalists saw kangaroos for the first time and they were amazed by this unusual animal. Sydney Parkinson drew beautiful colour pictures of the new animals and plants that were discovered during the voyage. Today you can see a lot of these drawings at the Natural History Museum in London.

After exploring Australia, Cook sailed north to what is now Jakarta in Indonesia and on to England, where he returned in July 1771 after a successful voyage of almost three years.

1. **claimed ... Britain** : 宣稱⋯為英屬
2. **darts** :

The Second Pacific Voyage (1772-75)

In July 1772 Cook led another expedition in search of the *Terra Australis* with two ships, the *Resolution* and the *Adventure.* He sailed south to the frozen continent of Antarctica, which he never really saw because of the terrible weather conditions and the large icebergs. No other explorer travelled so far south. He thought that the Southern Continent didn't exist, and continued exploring many other islands in the South Pacific: the Fiji Islands, Tonga, New Caledonia, Vanuatu and the Society Islands. On Easter Island he found some strange statues of men with big heads that were over 28 feet tall. The purpose of these statues is still a mystery and today they are a tourist attraction.

The Hawaiian coast.

The Third Pacific Voyage (1776-79)

When Cook returned to England in 1775 he was a national hero and became famous all over Europe. It was difficult for Cook to stay away from the sea, so in 1776 he led another expedition to find the Northwest Passage. For centuries explorers looked for a sea route north of Canada that connected the Atlantic and Pacific Oceans, but no one was able to find it.

Cook first sailed to Australia, New Zealand, Tonga and Tahiti with two ships, the *Resolution* and the *Discovery*. The local people received him and his crew with a huge welcome. Shortly after he began his voyage north and in January 1778 discovered a big group of islands that he called the Sandwich Islands. Today these islands are the American state of Hawaii.

He then sailed further north and explored and made maps of the Pacific coast from California

Hubbard Glacier in Seward, Alaska.

all the way to the Bering Strait in Alaska. He stopped at Nootka Sound, in Canada, where he bought fish, animal fat and fur from the local people. During this voyage the naturalists were able to see and draw polar bears, sea otters and walruses for the first time.

The weather conditions were very bad, but Cook bravely continued his voyage up the coast of Alaska to the Bering Strait, which separates Asia from North America. Although he tried to sail through the Bering Strait several times, the thick ice stopped him and damaged the *Resolution*. He could not find the Northwest Passage and returned to Hawaii to repair his ship. Unfortunately, in February 1779, he was killed in a fight with the local people.

The *Resolution* and the *Discovery* returned to Britain in October 1780. A young officer called William Bligh helped to bring Cook's ship back to Britain. Cook's many interesting discoveries and excellent maps were extremely useful to scientists, travellers and explorers. He became a national hero because of his courage and extraordinary navigation skills.

FACT FILE 知識檔案

Polynesians

The people Cook met during his voyages were Polynesians. It is believed that the Polynesian people were excellent navigators and came from South America centuries ago in small boats.

Scientists have found a lot of similarities between the people of South America and the Polynesians.

Polynesians can be divided into two main groups.

Western Polynesians: people who live in Tonga, Samoa, Niue and other Northwestern Polynesian Islands.

Eastern Polynesians: people who live in Tahiti, the Cook Islands, the Marquesas, Hawaii and Easter Island.

New Zealand was first settled by Eastern Polynesians called Maoris.

The text and **beyond**

1 Comprehension check
Complete the sentences (1-8) with their endings (A-H).

1 ☐ James Cook joined the Royal Navy in 1755
2 ☐ People believed that there was
3 ☐ On his first Pacific voyage
4 ☐ New Zealand's southern island
5 ☐ During Cook's third Pacific voyage
6 ☐ For the first time the naturalists
7 ☐ Captain Cook was not able to find
8 ☐ The *Resolution* and the *Discovery* returned to Britain in 1780

A a continent in the world's southern oceans.

B the Northwest Passage.

C he discovered the Sandwich Islands.

D and went on an expedition to Canada, where he stayed and made maps.

E without Captain Cook because he was killed in Hawaii during a fight.

F was discovered by Captain Cook.

G Captain Cook explored the eastern coast of Australia.

H saw polar bears, sea otters and walruses.

PET ② Sentence transformation

For each question complete the second sentence so that it means the same as the first. Use no more than three words. There is an example at the beginning. (0).

0 There was danger in sailing in the Arctic Ocean.
Sailing in the Arctic Ocean ...was dangerous... .

1 Captain Cook studied many maps and then travelled to the South Pacific.
Captain Cook studied many maps .... the South Pacific.

2 Joseph Banks was the only naturalist on the ship.
There was .... on the ship except Joseph Banks.

3 Sydney Parkinson drew a lot of pictures of new plants and animals.
A lot of pictures of new plants and animals .... Sydney Parkinson.

4 Captain Cook and his crew saw nothing except ice in Antarctica.
Captain Cook and his crew .... except ice in Antarctica.

T: GRADE 4

❸ Speaking: Work

The work of a sea captain was difficult and dangerous. He was not only responsible for the ship and the crew, but also for the success of the expedition. Talk to your partner about different kinds of work that are difficult and dangerous today. Use these questions to help you.

1 Why do people choose to do work that is difficult and dangerous?

2 Is there a kind of work that is difficult and dangerous and that you would like to do?

3 Why would you like to do it?

4 Would you be afraid or excited?

4 Captain William Bligh and the *Bounty*

Read the text and fill in the gaps with the past tense of the verbs in the box. The first has been done for you.

> lead   write   fail   try   die   ~~join~~   become
> learn   leave   sail   train   arrive

William Bligh was born in 1754 in the south-west of England and (0) ..joined. the British Royal Navy when he was a young boy. He then (1) .... to become an officer. At the age of twenty-two Bligh (2) .... with Captain Cook on the *Resolution* during his third and last Pacific voyage. After Captain Cook's death in Hawaii in 1779, Bligh helped to bring the *Resolution* back to Britain. He was an intelligent man and (3) .... a lot about navigation and map making from Captain Cook. In 1787 he (4) .... the captain of the *Bounty*, and (5) .... an expedition to Tahiti to collect breadfruit plants and take them to the Caribbean Islands. The crew was small and Fletcher Christian, a young man from a rich family, was second in command. The sea voyage to Tahiti was long and difficult because of stormy weather. When Bligh and his crew (6) .... in Tahiti they had to wait five months for the breadfruit plants to be ready to be taken on board the *Bounty*. The *Bounty* (7) .... Tahiti in April 1789 with an unhappy crew, because Bligh was a strict captain. Three weeks later Christian led a mutiny to take over the ship, because he and many other men wanted to go back to Tahiti. Bligh was very angry, and he and a few others (8) .... to stop the mutiny, but they (9) .... This event was called the Mutiny on the *Bounty*. Captain Bligh and eighteen men were put into a small boat with little food and water, a sextant, a watch but no map. Bligh was a very brave man and an excellent navigator, and after forty-seven days he was able to get to the island of Timor in Indonesia, after sailing 4,164 miles (6,701 km). Only one man (10) .... during the voyage. Bligh and the other men finally returned to Britain in March 1790. He (11) .... a book about the mutiny called *A Narrative of the Mutiny on Board His Majesty's Ship 'Bounty'.*
The mutineers could not go back to Britain, so they went to live on Pitcairn Island, a very small island south-east of Tahiti. Today about fifty people still live on Pitcairn Island.

INTERNET PROJECT

Let's find out more about Hawaii!

Go to www.blackcat-cideb.com. Insert the title or part of the title of this book into our search engine. Open the page for *Exploring Places*. Click on the Internet project link. Go down the page until you find the title of this book and click on the relevant link for this project.

Barack Obama, the 44th President of the United States of America, was born in Hawaii. Make a brief fact file about Hawaii by answering the following questions.

1 What is the capital and the largest city?
2 How many people live in the state of Hawaii?
3 What are the major industries?
4 Name the main islands that make up the state.
5 In your opinion, what is unusual about Hawaii?
6 Plan a seven-day vacation in Hawaii. What would you like to do and see? Compare your vacation plan with a partner.

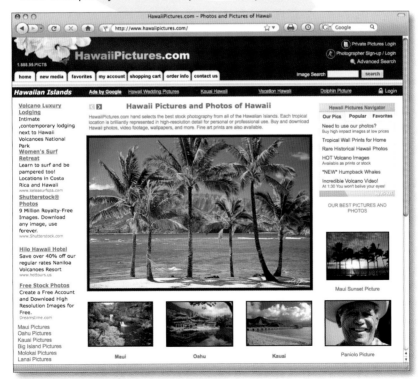

The Story of Maps 地圖的故事

Maps of the Earth were a part of human history for a long time, probably eight thousand years. But the oldest maps were of the skies, not of the Earth. Dots [1] found on the walls of the ancient Lascaux caves [2] show part of the night sky with three of the brightest stars, Altair, Deneb and Vega. These stars form the constellation of Summer Triangle in the skies of the northern hemisphere.

Ancient maps

People made and used maps when they started exploring the Earth. They made maps before they had a written language. The oldest picture that looks like a map was created about 9,000 years ago and found in Catalhoyuk, Turkey; it was the map of a village.

More than 6,000 years later a map was made in Babylonia. It is a small clay tablet [3] with a river and a valley between two hills. This map also showed the cardinal directions: North, South, East and West. The ancient Egyptians also made maps that showed the Nile Valley and the route to the gold mines of Nubia, part of ancient Ethiopia.

1. a dot : • ◄———
2. **Lascaux caves** : 拉斯科洞穴
3. **a clay tablet** : 泥板

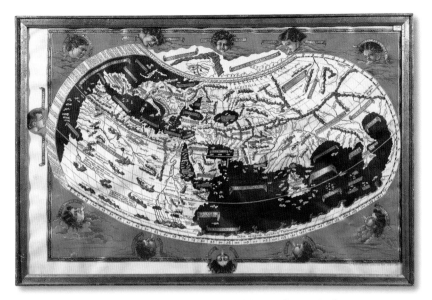

Facsimile of a fifteenth-century map of the world according to Ptolemy.

In the early 300s BCE the Greeks made maps of where they lived, and they were the first people to realise that the world was round. Around 330 BCE Aristotle noticed that when a ship was at the horizon its lower part was invisible [1]. This made him understand that the Earth was round and not flat.

The Romans [2] were the first to make road maps which helped them to travel around their huge empire. The most famous ancient maps were made by Ptolemy, an Egyptian scholar who lived in Alexandria, Egypt, about 150 CE. Like the Greeks, he believed that the world was round. He wrote the famous work *Geographica*, a collection of eight books with maps and information about the geography of the world during the Roman Empire in the second century. The first book was a collection of written information, and the other books

1. **invisible** : 不可見
2. **the Romans** : 羅馬人

Portolano showing Venice, Genoa and Marseille (15th century).

were atlases [1]. His maps were the first to have longitudinal and latitudinal lines [2]. Ptolemy's *Geographica* was first printed in Bologna, Italy in 1477.

In the 1300s and 1400s the *portolano* (from the Latin word *portus* meaning port) or navigator's chart, was used to navigate along the coasts of the Mediterranean Sea. This kind of map showed only the coasts and ports.

After Columbus's voyage to the New World, map makers all over the world had to change their maps. Almost every voyage of exploration had a map-maker who drew maps of the coast lines and islands to record the discoveries that were made. Scholars and cartographers [3] then added the latest discoveries to their atlases.

Famous map makers

Martin Behaim (1459-1507), a German navigator and astronomer, made the oldest existing globe [4] of the world in 1492, which you can see at the museum in Nuremberg, Germany.

1. **atlases** : 地圖集
2. **longitudinal and latitudinal lines** : 經線和緯線
3. **cartographers** : 製圖師
4. **globe** :

One of the great map makers of the 1500s was the Flemish [1] cartographer Gerardus Mercator. He made some of the best maps and globes of his time. In 1569 he was able to make a large map of the world, which measured 80 inches by 49 inches (202 cm by 124 cm) and was printed on eighteen pieces of paper. His maps were very useful to explorers.

The first map of the British colonies in America was a map of Virginia made by John Smith, who was the leader

1. **Flemish**：佛萊明

John Smith's Map of Virginia, 1624.

of the Jamestown colony in 1607. Smith also went to the New England colonies further north on the coast of America and made the first map of the area. These maps were published in England in 1612 and encouraged people to go to the New World.

Today map-makers use computer graphics programs to help them make all kinds of excellent maps and atlases. With the help of satellites we can see detailed maps of the entire world on our computers.

1 Comprehension check

Are the following statements true (T) or false (F)? Correct the false ones.

	T	F
1 There are ancient maps of the skies in the Lascaux Caves.	☐	☐
2 People made maps after having a written language.	☐	☐
3 The Babylonians drew maps on the walls of their homes.	☐	☐
4 The Greeks believed that the world was flat.	☐	☐
5 Ptolemy's *Geographica* was first printed in the fifteenth century.	☐	☐
6 The *portolano* was useful to navigators who crossed the Atlantic Ocean.	☐	☐
7 Gerardus Mercator was the greatest cartographer of the sixteenth century.	☐	☐

Before you read

1 Vocabulary

Match the pictures (A-F) with the words (1-6). Use a dictionary to help you.

1	herds of buffalo	4	pioneers
2	grizzly bear	5	dugout canoe
3	log fort	6	prairie dog

CHAPTER FOUR

The Lewis and Clark Expedition

開拓之旅

The Lewis and Clark Expedition opened the doors to the West and was responsible for the rapid growth of the United States.

In 1803 the American President Thomas Jefferson bought a huge piece of land from France for $15 million: the Louisiana Purchase. It went from the Mississippi River to the Rocky Mountains. No one knew exactly how big the land was, so President Jefferson asked Meriwether Lewis, his private secretary, and William Clark to explore it. They were both young, adventurous Army officers. Their job was to bring back detailed maps about the land and the Missouri River, and information about the American Indian tribes [1] and the wildlife of the area.

---

1. **tribes** : 部落

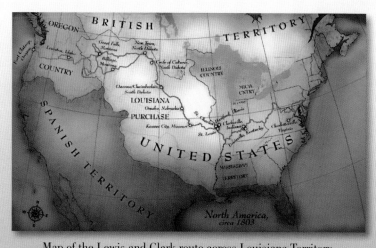

Map of the Lewis and Clark route across Louisiana Territory.

The expedition begins

Meriwether Lewis was a quiet man with a great interest in plants and animals. William Clark was a friendly man and an excellent hunter and map-maker. Lewis bought the supplies and organized the expedition, while Clark found the men for the journey and trained them. Lewis and Clark kept detailed diaries of their 8,000-mile expedition.

Lewis, Clark and about fifty men began the long journey in St Louis, Missouri in the spring of 1804. The expedition sailed up the Missouri River and crossed the Great Plains of North America, where the states of Missouri and Nebraska are today. Here they saw many herds of buffalo and wild horses. During the last week of August, Lewis and Clark reached the edge of the Great Plains; they were entering the territory of the Sioux Indians.

The first tribe they met was the Yankton Sioux, who were friendly, but disappointed by the small gifts they received from Lewis and Clark. The tribe warned them about the unfriendly Teton Sioux Indians who lived further west on the Missouri River.

Lewis and Clark met a Teton Sioux chief who wanted one of the expedition's boats, but they refused. The Teton Sioux tribe became angry and the men of the expedition were ready to fight. Fortunately, at the last moment, nobody wanted to fight, and the expedition continued its journey towards the West. The journey was difficult and dangerous, and the men were sometimes attacked by grizzly bears.

Lewis and Clark meet Sacagawea

When they reached what is now North Dakota, the freezing winter weather stopped them. They were in the territory of the Mandan Indian tribe, who were friendly and helpful. They built a log fort and called it Fort Mandan. They stayed there and waited for warmer weather before continuing their journey. At Fort Mandan, Lewis and Clark met a French-Canadian fur trapper [1] called Toussaint Charbonneau, whose young wife was a Shoshone Indian. Lewis and Clark decided to employ them because Charbonneau knew the territory well and his wife, Sacagawea, spoke several American Indian languages.

In the spring of 1805 they built a boat and continued travelling up the Missouri River, but the journey became more difficult because the river currents [2] were very strong. When

1. **fur trapper** : 皮草商
2. **currents** : 水流

Sacagawea Guiding the Lewis and Clark Expedition (about 1904) by Alfred Russell.

they reached a huge waterfall, known as the Great Falls, they had to travel around it and carry all their equipment. The tall Rocky Mountains were the next big difficulty.

Sacagawea's people were the friendly Shoshone Indians, who lived in the Rocky Mountains. They were happy to see her and gave Lewis and Clark the horses they needed to cross the mountains. Sacagawea knew the area well and guided the expedition through an important mountain pass called the Lehmi Pass. The expedition then made dug-out canoes and continued travelling west down the Snake and the Columbia Rivers. On 7 November 1805 the expedition finally reached their goal: the Pacific Ocean! This is what Clark wrote in his diary: 'Ocean in view! Oh! The joy!'

Sketches by William Clark in the Lewis
and Clark expedition diary.

The expedition built Fort Clatsop on the south side of the Columbia River and spent the cold, rainy winter there. During the winter months the men became friendly with the local American Indian tribes and learned more about the Pacific Coast.

On 23 March 1806 the expedition left Fort Clatsop and began the long journey home. After several difficulties with the Blackfeet and the Crow Indians, the men reached St Louis, Missouri on 23 September 1806, and were greeted like heroes.

The expedition was a great success and the most important in American history. Lewis and Clark prepared about 140 detailed maps and they kept records of over 100 different kinds of animals and about 176 plants. They brought President Jefferson a new kind of animal as a gift: a live prairie dog.

Lewis and Clark opened the doors to the West. With good maps and knowledge of the land, the first pioneers [1] in their covered wagons started travelling to the new territories and the United States began growing.

1. **pioneers** : 先驅

FACT FILE 知識檔案

Native Americans or American Indians

Scientists believe that the American Indians came from Asia about 15,000 years ago by crossing the Bering Strait, which was then a natural land bridge.

They settled in North, Central and South America, and lived in different tribes, each with a chief. They lived by hunting, fishing and farming.

Some of the main tribes were the Sioux, the Cheyenne, the Comanche, the Apache, the Navajo, the Shoshone, the Chumash, the Pomo, the Iroquois and the Seminole. They were a great people who lived in harmony with nature.

The text and **beyond**

1 **Comprehension check**

Read the text below and choose the correct answer for each space —
A, B, C or D. The first has been done for you (0)

Meriwether Lewis and William Clark were asked (0) ...C... President
Jefferson to explore the Louisiana Purchase and bring (1) ....
information about the land, American Indian tribes and wildlife.
The expedition of about fifty men left St Louis, Missouri (2) ....
the spring of 1804. They sailed up the Missouri River and crossed
the great plains where they saw (3) .... herds of buffalo. They met
a Teton Sioux chief (4) .... wanted one of the expedition's boats,
but Lewis and Clark refused. Their journey (5) .... the West was
difficult and often dangerous. (6) .... the freezing winter of 1804,
the expedition stopped in the Mandan Indian territory and built a
fort called Fort Mandan. Here Lewis and Clark met a fur trapper and
his American Indian wife, Sacagawea. Lewis and Clark decided to
(7) .... them, because the fur trapper knew the territory (8) ....
and his wife spoke several Indian languages.
The expedition reached the Pacific Ocean on 7 November 1805
and built Fort Clatsop on the Columbia River. When they (9) ....
returned to St Louis in 1806 everyone was happy to see them. Their
maps and diaries were extremely (10) .... to President Jefferson
and the pioneers who wanted to go and live in the new territories.

0	**A** to	**B** at	**C** by	**D** for
1	**A** back	**B** about	**C** up	**D** down
2	**A** near	**B** at	**C** on	**D** in
3	**A** much	**B** many	**C** very	**D** lots
4	**A** who	**B** that	**C** which	**D** he
5	**A** at	**B** towards	**C** about	**D** near
6	**A** Through	**B** While	**C** During	**D** Around
7	**A** carry	**B** work	**C** job	**D** employ
8	**A** good	**B** well	**C** better	**D** best
9	**A** last	**B** final	**C** finally	**D** lastly
10	**A** usefully	**B** used	**C** use	**D** useful

 **Listening**

PET

Listen to the story about the first pioneers. Choose the correct picture and put a tick (✓) below it — A, B or C.

1 When did the pioneers begin their journey to the West?

A   B   C

2 What was the biggest difficulty?

A   B   C

3 What did the pioneers lack in the summer?

  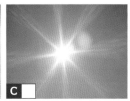

A   B   C

4 When did the pioneers choose a campsite?

  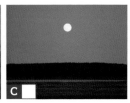

A   B   C

 **③ Writing**

Imagine you are Meriwether Lewis and write about 35-45 words in your diary about:

- the freezing winter weather in Mandan territory
- the building of Fort Mandan
- the fur trapper and his wife.

Start like this:

We didn't expect this terribly cold weather...

INTERNET PROJECT

Let's visit the Lewis and Clark National Historic Park!

Divide the class into three groups; each group can prepare a brief fact file on one of the following:

- Fort Clatsop and Fort to Sea Trail
- Station Camp
- The Salt Works and Netul Landing.

Discuss your fact file with the other groups.

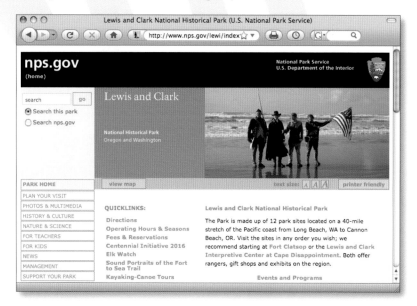

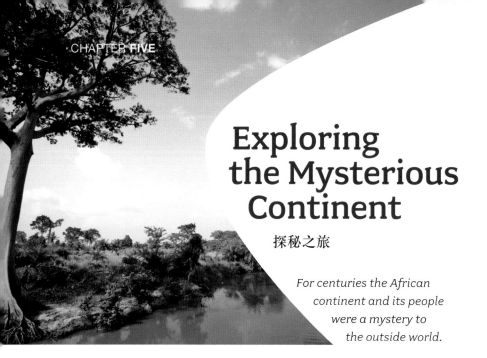

CHAPTER FIVE

Exploring the Mysterious Continent

探秘之旅

For centuries the African continent and its people were a mystery to the outside world.

For centuries people traded with African merchants who lived north of the Sahara Desert and along the east and west coasts of Africa. But in the early 19th century the huge interior [1] of the African continent was unknown to the outside world. It was extremely difficult to travel to the interior of Africa because of its geography and climate. People called it the mysterious continent because so little was known about it.

Speke and Burton

John Speke was an officer in the British Army who made three exploratory voyages to Africa to look for the source of the Nile River. In 1856 he joined the famous British explorer, Sir Richard

---

1. **interior** : 内部

Scene from the film *Mountains of the Moon* (1990) directed by Bob Rafelson.

Francis Burton, on an expedition to East Africa to find the great lakes that people talked about. After a long and extremely difficult journey during which both men became ill with tropical diseases, they became the first Europeans to discover Lake Tanganyika. They heard of a second lake in the area, but Burton was too ill to travel. So Speke went alone with his African carriers [1] and found a huge lake, which he identified correctly as the source of the River Nile. He called it Lake Victoria in honour of the British Queen Victoria. However, a lot of Speke's equipment and diaries got lost during the difficult journey, so there aren't many written details about his discovery.

1. **carriers** : 搬運工

Livingstone and Stanley

In the middle of the 19th century European missionaries [1] went to work in little-known areas of Africa; sometimes they became explorers and traders. In 1841 David Livingstone, an adventurous Scottish missionary, started working north of the Orange River in South Africa. He was interested in science and nature, and wanted to find out more about Africa and its people.

From 1852 to 1856 Livingstone and his carriers travelled about 5,600 miles (9,000 km) across the African continent, from Luanda on the Atlantic Ocean to Quelimane on the Indian Ocean. He was one of the first Europeans to make this difficult transcontinental journey through the thick tropical forests, meeting all kinds of danger. In November 1855 he discovered a huge waterfall in southern Africa, on the River Zambezi, between

1. **missionary/missionaries** : 傳教士
    1 mile = 1.60935 km

Victoria Falls.

what is now Zambia and Zimbabwe. He called it Victoria Falls and this is what he wrote in his diary about his discovery: '*No one can imagine the beauty of the view...*'

Victoria Falls is one of the largest waterfalls in the world and it attracts thousands of tourists every year. It is a UNESCO World Heritage Site.

Map of South Africa showing the routes of Livingstone between the years 1848-56.

Livingstone returned to England for some time and then left again for Africa, because he wanted to explore other parts of the continent. In 1866 he began looking for the source of the Nile River, since he disagreed with Speke's idea that it was Lake Victoria. He reached the southern part of Lake Tanganyika and continued looking for the source of the Nile. During this difficult expedition he became very ill, and much of his equipment was stolen. He lost contact with the rest of the world and no one knew where he was.

Stanley was born in Wales, Great Britain in 1841, but he emigrated to the USA in 1859. He became a journalist for the *New York Herald*, and in 1869 the newspaper sent him to look for Livingstone. He arrived in Zanzibar, an island on the east coast of Africa, at the beginning of 1871. The 701-mile expedition through the African jungle was extremely difficult; tropical diseases killed many of his carriers and his horse. Finally on 10 November 1871 Stanley found Livingstone, who was weak and ill, at Ujiji, near

'Dr Livingstone, I Presume?': the meeting of Stanley and Livingstone at Ujiji in 1871.

Lake Tanganyika. When the two men met, Stanley spoke the words which have become famous, 'Dr Livingstone, I presume [1]?'

The food and medicine that Stanley brought helped Livingstone to get better, and together they soon started exploring Lake Tanganyika by boat. When Stanley left Africa, Livingstone refused to join him because he wanted to continue exploring. He died of fever in 1873. During his adventurous life he travelled more than 28, 993 miles in Africa and made maps of almost 1,609,351 square miles. After his death, he was given a gold medal from the British Royal Geographical Society for his explorations.

Congo River.

1. **presume**：假定

In 1874 the *New York Herald* and Britain's *Daily Telegraph* financed Stanley on another expedition to Africa: he had to find the course of the River Congo to the sea. This was an extremely difficult expedition because the River Congo is the second longest river in Africa after the Nile. Stanley spent a lot of time organizing the expedition. During the journey down the long river he and his men were often attacked by native tribes. On 9 August 1877, after 999 days, the expedition reached the mouth of the River Congo.

When Stanley finally returned to Great Britain in 1892 he was greeted as a hero. He became a member of Parliament from 1895 to 1900 and died in 1904.

Mary Kingsley

Mary Kingsley was an English explorer and writer who greatly influenced European ideas about Africa and its people. She was born in London in 1862 and as a young woman she spent a lot of her time at home looking after her invalid [1] parents. Although she did not go to school, Mary loved reading scientific and geographical books from her father's library: he was an explorer and travel writer, too.

When her parents died in 1892, she decided to visit Africa to collect material for her father's unfinished book about the mysterious continent. This was a brave decision because women in Victorian days did not travel to other parts of the world alone

1. **invalid** : 久病的

— and certainly not to Africa! Her friends were worried about this trip and tried to stop her. But no one could stop Mary Kingsley.

She arrived in Luanda in Angola, West Africa in August 1893, and with a small team of African carriers she travelled inland. West Africa was unknown to Europeans at that time. She followed the River Congo into the tropical jungle and was fascinated by the people and the wildlife. In 1894 she returned to England with many specimens of insects and river fish, which she took to the Natural History Museum in London.

Mary loved Africa and the following year she went back. This time she went to Gabon, a country north of Angola. She travelled up the River Ogooué and was the first European to visit certain parts of inland Gabon. For several months she lived peacefully with the Fang tribe, who were cannibals [1]. When she first saw the Fang people, Mary and her carriers held out their empty hands to show that they had no weapons [2]. They came in peace and the Fang people understood this and welcomed them.

Kingsley made friends with the people of different tribes, who taught her how to live in the jungle and travel down a river in

1. **cannibals** : 食人族
2. **weapons** :

Mary Kingsley sitting in a canoe travelling on the Ogowe River.

a canoe. She collected many specimens of previously unknown fish. She climbed the tallest mountain of West Africa, Mount Cameroon (13,760 feet — 4,400 metres), by a route unknown to other Europeans. She travelled through Africa dressed in a long black dress with a pair of her brother's trousers underneath.

When she returned to England in October 1895 she was a popular figure and many journalists wanted to interview her. For three years she toured Britain and talked about life in Africa. She did not agree with the missionaries who wanted to change the people of Africa. She defended the African way of life and asked others to accept and appreciate the differences between cultures. Most people in Victorian England did not agree with her.

Kingsley wrote two books about her experiences: *Travels in West Africa* (1897), which was a best-seller, and *West African Studies* (1899). During the Boer War [1], Kingsley went to work as a nurse in South Africa, where she died of fever in 1900.

FACT FILE 知識檔案

Forgotten heroes

African guides and carriers were very important during all expeditions. A big expedition usually had more than 300 paid African workers who were organized by a team leader called a *kirangazi*. They carried heavy equipment, supplies, boats and other objects during the journey. When the expeditions leaders were ill or injured, they carried them, too! The most famous *kirangazi* was nicknamed 'Bombay', and he was part of Speke's expeditions.

1. **Boer War**：波耳戰

The text and **beyond**

PET ① **Comprehension check**

For each question choose the correct answer — A, B, C or D.

1 What did Speke and Burton discover together?
   - A ☐ Lake Victoria
   - B ☐ East Africa
   - C ☐ the Nile River
   - D ☐ Lake Tanganyika

2 Who discovered the lake that was the source of the River Nile?
   - A ☐ John Speke
   - B ☐ Sir Richard Francis Burton
   - C ☐ Speke and Burton
   - D ☐ an unknown British explorer

3 David Livingstone was a Scottish missionary who
   - A ☐ became an explorer and discovered Victoria Falls.
   - B ☐ discovered the River Zambezi.
   - C ☐ explored the Orange River in South Africa.
   - D ☐ worked for the *New York Herald*.

4 Henry Stanley went on a 700-mile expedition in Africa
   - A ☐ and then died of a tropical fever.
   - B ☐ and received a Gold Medal.
   - C ☐ down the River Congo.
   - D ☐ to look for Livingstone, who was missing.

5 Lake Tanganyika was explored
   - A ☐ by Mary Kingsley and her African carriers.
   - B ☐ by boat by Stanley and Livingstone.
   - C ☐ by Livingstone and other missionaries.
   - D ☐ by Speke and Burton.

6 Mary Kingsley left Britain in 1892 and travelled to Africa
   - A ☐ but never returned.
   - B ☐ to find material for her father's book.
   - C ☐ to meet the Fang tribe.
   - D ☐ to work as a missionary.

PET ② Notes and notices

Look at the text in each question. What does it say? Mark the correct letter — A, B or C.

1

> ZANZIBAR BEACH
> HOTEL
> Guests are requested to
> hand in all keys at the desk
> when they check out

A ☐ Pick up your keys at the desk when you arrive.

B ☐ When you leave the hotel give in your keys at the desk.

C ☐ If you lose your keys, pay for them at the desk.

2

> LAKE TANGANYIKA
> BOAT RIDE
> Euro 10 per person
> Children pay half price if
> accompanied by parents

A ☐ Children must be accompanied by parents.

B ☐ Children pay 5 Euros.

C ☐ Only children can take the boat ride.

3

> **Victoria Falls**
>
> **For you own safety
> please queue on
> other side**

A ☐ It is safer to wait in a queue on the other side.

B ☐ Queue on the other side for information about safety.

C ☐ It is dangerous to queue on the other side.

4

> SAFARI SHOE SHOP
> SORRY! WE ARE
> CLOSED FOR REPAIRS.
> WE REOPEN ON
> SATURDAY.

A ☐ Repair work begins on Saturday.

B ☐ Repair work is being done until Saturday.

C ☐ The shop does repair work.

5

> **Nile River Cruise
> Office**
> *Ring bell for attention.*
> Office opens at 9.30 am

A ☐ Don't ring the bell before 9.30.

B ☐ The office will open before 9.30 if you ring the bell.

C ☐ After 9.30, ring the bell and someone will help you.

INTERNET PROJECT

Let's visit Victoria Falls National Park!

Work with a partner and answer the following questions.

1 How tall are Victoria Falls?
2 How wide are they?
3 Why do Africans call the falls *mosi-oa-tunya*?
4 What surrounds the falls?
5 What animals can you see there?
6 Which countries share Victoria Falls?

Before you read

1 **Vocabulary**

Match the pictures (A-D) with the words (1-4).

1 sledge   2 pony   3 Inuit   4 ice-cap

A

B

C

D

CHAPTER SIX

The Race to the Poles

極地探險

*The extreme climate
and the difficult position
of the Poles discouraged
many explorers.*

In December 1839 a United States Navy expedition called the Wilkes Expedition sailed from Sydney, Australia and reported the discovery of the Antarctic continent which Captain Cook looked for years before. Now all the continents of the world were discovered.

By the late 19th century scientists had some information about the North and South Poles. They knew about ice-caps and how they were formed, kept records of polar weather and had maps of the Arctic and Antarctic boundaries. However, no one was able to reach the North or the South Pole. At this time the governments of the world were starting to finance scientific explorations and so the 'race to the poles' became a matter of national pride [1].

---

1.   **pride** : 自豪感

Roald Amundsen

Roald Amundsen became the most successful of all Polar explorers. He was born in Norway in 1872 and as a young man he was fascinated by the stories he read about explorers and wanted to become one. He slept with open windows during the very cold Norwegian winters to train himself. In 1897 he joined an expedition to the Antarctic but he did not travel far inland. This was a great experience which he enjoyed very much.

In 1903 Amundsen led the first successful expedition to the Northwest Passage on the ship *Gjoa*. It took him nearly three years to complete this journey, because he and his crew could only sail when the pack-ice [1] melted. Amundsen and his men sailed from Norway up the west coast of Greenland into Baffin Bay. Then he sailed through Barrow Strait and spent the winter on one of the Canadian islands.

During this time he and his men travelled by dog-sledge and were able to find the exact position of the North Magnetic Pole [2]. He also made friends with the local Inuit people who taught him how to live in the Arctic. He learned to use sledges pulled by dogs to travel in the snow and ice, and to wear light animal skins, instead

---

1. **pack-ice**：海冰
2. **North Magnetic Pole**：北磁極

Inuit family (about 1920).

of heavy, woollen clothing. In 1905 Amundsen and his men sailed to the Beaufort Sea, through the Bering Strait and successfully landed in Alaska. By doing this, Amundsen became the first person to navigate the Northwest Passage, which explorers tried to do since the time of Columbus.

During 1905 Norway became independent of Sweden and had a new king. Amundsen loved his country and wrote to King Haakon VII and told him about his expedition. He said that his explorations were a great achievement for Norway and that he hoped to do more for his country.

After navigating the Northwest Passage, Amundsen wanted to go to the North Pole and explore it. But he heard that the American explorer Frederick Cook reached the North Pole in April 1908, and then Robert Peary, another American explorer, reached the North Pole in April 1909, so he decided not to go.

At this point Amundsen decided to explore Antarctica and reach the South Pole, because he had a lot of experience with travelling and living in freezing weather conditions. Antarctica is rich in natural beauty and has unusual wild life, but its geography and weather are much worse than the North Pole. There are high mountains covered with very hard ice and extremely strong winds and snow storms.

Robert Scott enters the race

Amundsen was clever and he did not tell anyone about his plans, because he knew he was entering a race. The British explorer Robert Scott was also leading an expedition to Antarctica and the South Pole. Amundsen wanted to get to the South Pole first.

On 3 June 1910 Amundsen and his men left Oslo, Norway on the ship *Fram,* which means 'forward' in Norwegian. When he got to the Portuguese islands of Madeira, he sent a telegram to Scott that said: 'Beg to inform you FRAM proceeding Antarctic — Amundsen'.

The *Fram.*

Amundsen's expedition landed in the Bay of Whales, Antarctica on 14 January 1911 and a camp was set up immediately. This camp was 60 miles (97 km) closer to the South Pole than Scott's camp. Amundsen and his men wore light Inuit-type skins and used dog-sledges and skis to travel around. Amundsen's men were well trained and they travelled with little equipment.

In October 1911, during the Antarctic spring, Amundsen and four of his best men started going to the South Pole. They travelled much faster than Scott's group because they used sledges pulled by dogs. Scott used sledges pulled by ponies and motor sledges. Ponies did not travel well in the snow and ice, and got hurt easily. When they were hurt, they had to be shot. Motor sledges soon broke down and Scott's men pulled the sledges themselves. This was extremely tiring and they moved slowly.

On 14 December 1911 Amundsen and his men reached the South Pole, thirty-five days before Scott's group. Amundsen and his men were the first people to reach the South

Amundsen's arrival at the South Pole, 1911.

Pole and they raised a Norwegian flag there. Amundsen took only two photographs of the great event. He and his men returned safely to their camp on 25 January 1912, but did not make a public announcement about the expedition's success until they arrived at Hobart in Tasmania, Australia in March 1912.

When Scott and his men reached the South Pole on 17 January 1912, they realized that Amundsen got there before them because they saw the Norwegian flag and found sledge tracks and signs of dogs paws in the ice. Scott and his men were very upset. This is what Scott wrote in his diary: 'The Norwegians have forestalled us [1] and are first at the Pole. It is a terrible disappointment... all the daydreams must go. Great God! This is an awful place.'

Scott and his men began their long return trip back to the camp, but terrible weather conditions and poor health stopped them. Unfortunately, these brave men died on their return journey from the South Pole. Their frozen bodies and diaries were found many months later.

In 1918 Amundsen returned to the Arctic and led an expedition that sailed through the Northeast Passage. This was a route to the north of Russia that navigators tried to find for centuries.

1.　**forestalled us** : 防止我們

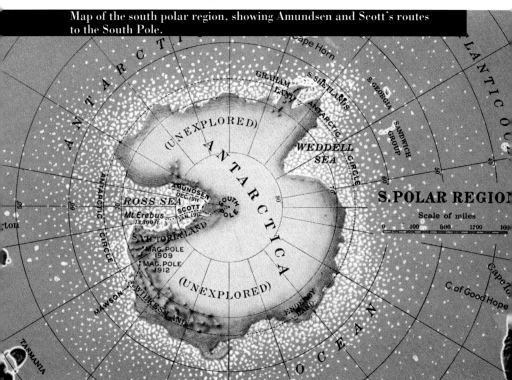

Map of the south polar region, showing Amundsen and Scott's routes to the South Pole.

Roald Amundsen monument, Tromso (Norway).

His last great achievement was his flight over the North Pole in an airplane, the *Norge,* in 1926. Two years later he disappeared in the Arctic while flying an airplane to try to find an airship [1] pilot who crashed in the ice. Amundsen's body was never found; he was one of the greatest explorers of the 20th century.

Today the North and South Poles are often the sites of races, marathons and endurance tests [2]. People who take part in them are much better equipped and prepared than Amundsen and Scott. In April 2007 the first North Pole Marathon took place. There were 43 athletes from 22 nations who ran around the top of the world for 26 miles, with a temperature of -25°C. The

1. **an airship**：飛艇

2. **endurance tests**：耐力測試

winner of this unusual marathon was Thomas Maguire from Ireland, who ran for 3 hours and 36 minutes.

The first South Pole Marathon took place in 2005 and there is one every year. Often these marathons and endurance tests are done for charity or to call attention to a good cause.

FACT FILE 知識檔案

The Inuits

The Inuits are a people who live in the Arctic areas of Canada, Greenland and Alaska. Their culture was born in western Alaska around 1000 CE and spread east across the Arctic. They are hunters and fishermen and travel with dog sledges. In winter they live in igloos, which are small houses made of snow and ice, and in summer they live in tents made of animal skins.

The text and **beyond**

Comprehension check

Read these sentences about Chapter Six. Decide if each sentence is correct or incorrect. If it correct, mark A. If it is not correct, mark B.

A   B

1   During the nineteenth century no one ever explored the North or South Pole.

2   Amundsen's journey to find the Northwest Passage took him almost three years.

3   Amundsen and his men left Norway on dog sledges.

4   Columbus was the first man to find the Northwest Passage and Amundsen took the same route.

5   The weather and geography of the North and South Poles are different.

6   The race to the South Pole was between Amundsen and Peary.

7   Amundsen sent a letter to Robert Scott telling him about his plan.

8   Amundsen and his men won the race to the South Pole because they knew how to live and travel in freezing weather conditions.

9   Robert Scott's diary and body were found after his death.

10   Amundsen and his airplane disappeared over the North Pole in 1926.

2 **Question words**

Fill in the gaps with the correct question word in the box. Then find the correct answers to the questions below (A-F).

> **When   How   Why   What   Who   Where**

1   .... are the Inuits? .....

2   .... was the name of the ship that took Amundsen to Antarctica? .....

3   .... did Amundsen set up a camp in Antarctica?. .....

4   .... did Scott reach the South Pole? .....

5   .... often does the South Pole Marathon take place? .....

6   .... did Amundsen and his men wear animals skins? .....

A   In the Bay of Whales.

B   They are the native people who live in Alaska and Canada.

C   Because they were light and very warm.

D   It takes place every year.

E   It was called the *Fram.*

F   On 17 January 1912.

'Amundsen and his men reached the South Pole thirty-five days before Scott's group.'

Time clauses are used to say when something happens by referring to a period of time or to another event.

Look at these examples:
*He wrote to his family **when** he reached Antarctica.*
*They started their trip to the mountains **before** it started snowing.*
*He wrote about his journey **while** he was sailing.*
*The dogs started running **as soon** as they saw the snow.*

3 Time clauses 時間從句
Complete the following sentences with a time clause from the box.

> before   as soon as   after   while   until

1   No one was able to discover the Antarctic continent .... the Wilkes expedition in 1839.
2   Amundsen learnt many things from the Inuit people .... living on a Canadian island.
3   .... leaving for the South Pole, Amundsen trained his men.
4   Scott got to the South Pole thirty-five days .... Amundsen.
5   .... Amundsen reached Hobart in Tasmania, Australia he made a public announcement about his expedition's success.

4 Who did what?
Match the person (A-F) with the correct description (1-10). You can use the same name more than once.

1   ☐   He reached the North Pole in April 1908.
2   ☐   His ship was called the *Fram*.
3   ☐   They discovered the continent of Antarctica.
4   ☐   He found the Northwest Passage.
5   ☐   He reached the North Pole in April 1909.
6   ☐   He used sledges pulled by ponies and motor sledges to travel in Antarctica.
7   ☐   His airplane was called the *Norge*.
8   ☐   They taught Amundsen how to live in the Arctic.
9   ☐   He was never able to return to his camp in Antarctica.
10 ☐   He was the winner of the 2007 North Pole Marathon.

A	The Inuits	E	Thomas Maguire
B	Roald Amundsen	F	The Wilkes Expedition
C	Frederick Cook	G	Robert Peary
D	Robert Scott		

INTERNET PROJECT

Let's find out more about Sir Ranulph Fiennes!

Sir Ranulph Fiennes is a British adventurer and according to the Guinness Book of World Records he is the world's greatest living adventurer. Many of his adventures and expeditions are for a good cause, like charity. Divide the class into four groups and each one can discuss:

- Everest Challenge 2009
- Exel North Pole expedition 2009
- Land Rover Global Expedition 1998
- About Ran.

Exploration in Films 電影中探險

There have been a great number of films about explorers, their lives and their exciting adventures. Audiences like finding out about men and women who have done great things.

The Vikings (1958), starring Kirk Douglas and Tony Curtis, is a great adventure film about two Viking half-brothers who don't know each other's identity. One brother is a brave warrior and the other is an ex-slave. They both want the throne of Northumbria in Britain and they fight for it. In the film you can see how the Vikings dressed, how they lived and how they fought; and there are excellent reconstructions [1] of the Viking longships.

1. **reconstructions** : 重建

The Vikings (1958) directed by Richard Fleischer.

Sir Francis Drake (1962), directed by Clive Donner, is a British TV series starring Terence Morgan. In twenty-six parts, it tells about the exciting life and surprising adventures both on land and at sea of the first Englishman to circumnavigate the world. There is an excellent reconstruction of Drake's ship, *Golden Hind,* and a part showing Drake fighting and defeating the Spanish Armada. Captain Cook's first voyage to the South Pacific and his discovery of the east coast of Australia is beautifully filmed in *Captain James Cook* (1987), a TV mini-series directed by Lawrence Gordon Clark, starring Keith Michell in the role of Captain Cook. Captain William Bligh, who sailed with Captain Cook during his third and last voyage to the South Pacific, is one of the protagonists in several 'Mutiny on the Bounty' films. The general public is attracted to the adventurous story of the *Bounty's* voyage, its crew and its mutiny.

Several films remember the Lewis and Clark expedition, but one of the best is a sixty-minute film by National Geographic Magazine, *Lewis and Clark: Great Journey West* (2002). It was filmed on location [1] in the Rocky Mountains, on the Columbia River and in the state of Washington.

The BBC's TV mini-series, *The Search for the Nile* (1971), directed by Richard Marquand, tells about the exciting adventures of John Speke and Sir Richard Francis Burton as they search for the source of the Nile River. The mini-series also tells about David Livingstone's amazing travels across the African continent, and how Henry Stanley searched for and found Livingstone. The series was filmed on location in Africa.

1.　**on location**：實景

The Red Tent (1969) directed by Mikhail Kalatozov.

Roald Amundsen and other North Pole explorers are remembered in *The Red Tent,* (1969), starring Sean Connery and Peter Finch. The film tells the story about an airship that crashed in the North Pole in 1928 and how Amundsen lost his life trying to find it.

The Last Place on Earth (1985), directed by Ferdinand Fairfax, is an adventurous British TV mini-series about Amundsen and Scott and the race to the South Pole, which was filmed in Greenland.

The French writer Jules Verne (1828-1905) wrote a series of fantasy exploration novels that inspired famous films that young people like a lot. *20,000 Leagues Under the Sea* (1954), starring James Mason and Kirk Douglas, was one of them. It was the first deep-sea adventure film and it was very successful. There are two film versions of Verne's exciting novel, *Journey to the Centre*

20.000 Leagues under the Sea (1954) directed by Mikhail Kalatozov.

of the Earth. The first version, directed by Henry Levi, came out in 1959 and the second, which is a science-fiction thriller, came out in 2008, directed by Eric Brevig. There are also two film versions of Verne's adventurous novel, *Around the World in Eighty Days.* The first, directed by Michael Anderson and starring David Niven, came out in 1956, and the second, directed by Frank Coraci, in 2004.

The Abyss (1989).

One of the most frightening deep-sea science-fiction films is *The Abyss* (1989), directed by James Cameron and starring Ed Harris. It tells about a group of divers who are looking for a lost submarine on the bottom of the ocean and the strange things that happen to them.

Academy-award winning director James Cameron also directed *Ghosts of the Abyss* (2003), a documentary [1] film that explores the wreckage [2] of the unfortunate ship

1. **documentary** : 紀錄
2. **wreckage** : 殘骸

78

Titanic, which lies on the bottom of the North Atlantic Ocean. Cameron was the director of the dramatic film *Titanic* (1997), which won eleven Academy Awards.

Star Trek is a very successful American science fiction series with eleven films and six TV series. It was created by Gene Roddenberry in 1966 and immediately became popular all over the world with audiences of all ages. The stories are set in outer space with the crew of the spaceship *Enterprise* in the middle of the 21st and 22nd centuries. *Star Trek* has won many important prizes, and the latest film of the series is *Star Trek* (2009).

Star Trek, first TV series (1966).

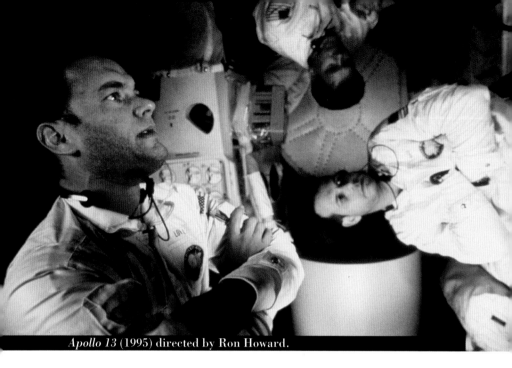

Apollo 13 (1995) directed by Ron Howard.

Apollo 13 (1995), starring Tom Hanks and Kevin Bacon, tells the true story of America's third moon-landing mission that met with a lot of mechanical problems. The film is dramatic because the three astronauts were in great danger in outer space. Fortunately, they were able to return to Earth safely. The film won two Academy Awards and several other prizes.

1 Comprehension check
Answer the following questions.

1 Which films show historical events and which ones are fiction?

2 Where was *Lewis and Clark: Great Journey West* filmed?

3 What is *The Red Tent* about?

4 Who was Jules Verne and which of his books became films?

5 Which film takes place on the bottom of the ocean?

6 What is *Star Trek*?

7 Which true story won two Academy Awards?

8 Talk about your favourite film on exploration with your partner.

Before you read

① Listening

PET

Listen to the first part of Chapter Seven and choose the correct anwer — A, B or C.

1   Who built the first submarine?

 A ☐ Edmond Halley

 B ☐ David Bushnell

 C ☐ Luigi Marsigli

2   Who was Luigi Marsigli?

 A ☐ An Italian inventor.

 B ☐ An Italian engineer.

 C ☐ An Italian naturalist.

3   What was *The Turtle*?

 A ☐ The first submarine.

 B ☐ The first diving bell with a window.

 C ☐ The first diving suit.

4   Where did the British ship *HMS Challenger* sail?

 A ☐ To the Mediterranean Sea.

 B ☐ To the Arctic Ocean.

 C ☐ To every ocean in the world except the Arctic.

5   What can be found on the ocean floor?

 A ☐ Natural gas and petroleum.

 B ☐ Submarines.

 C ☐ Nothing.

CHAPTER SEVEN

The Ocean Bottom and the Final Frontier: Space 上天下海

The bottom of the ocean and outer space are man's last frontiers.

About three-quarters of the earth's surface is covered by water. For centuries people asked questions like 'How deep is the ocean?' or 'What creatures live there?' Their questions remained unanswered for a long time. Navigators and explorers sailed the oceans and made maps that showed coastlines, seas, oceans and bodies of land. But there was no way of exploring *underwater*.

Underwater explorers need two things: a continuous air supply to breathe and protection from the great water pressure [1] that is above them. Divers need special clothing and light, since deep waters are very cold and very dark because the sun's rays cannot reach there. Underwater work and exploration is dangerous and today robots are used for many explorations.

1. **pressure** : 壓力

The beginning of oceanography [1]

In 1690 the British scientist Edmond Halley built a diving bell with a window that allowed men to work underwater. Extra air was sent in through leather pipes. Halley and five other men dived to 60 feet in the River Thames and stayed there for over ninety minutes. He improved the diving bell and was later able to stay underwater up to four hours.

In 1706 the Italian naturalist Luigi Marsigli was the first underwater explorer; he worked off the coast of southern France. He had very little equipment, but he was able to study the sea and wrote about it. He is the founder of modern oceanography.

In 1775 the American inventor David Bushnell invented the first submarine called *The Turtle*. It was quite small and there was only space for one man. *The Turtle* was first used during the American Revolution in 1776 against the British Navy on the coast of New York City.

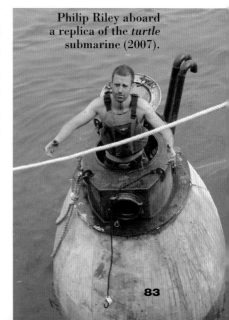

Philip Riley aboard a replica of the *turtle* submarine (2007).

1. **oceanography**：海洋學

Augustus Siebe was a German-born British engineer who invented the diving suit in 1819. Air was sent into the helmet of the diver by a long tube. By 1837 he developed a waterproof [1] diving suit that was used for many years by divers.

The British ship *HMS* [2] *Challenger* was the first ship especially designed for deep-sea exploration, with a complete laboratory for scientific work. Between 1872-1876 the ship sailed to every ocean in the world except the Arctic.

On 21 December 1872 Captain George Nares and his crew sailed on *HMS Challenger* from Portsmouth, England and travelled for 731 days at sea. The expedition studied sea water and sea life, and made detailed maps of the coastlines and islands. It also measured the depth of the sea in many different places, using the sounding weight.

The expedition found over 4,700 unknown species of sea life and brought back a great amount of useful information. The *Challenger* returned to England on 24 May 1876 after having sailed for nearly 70,000 nautical miles.

1. **waterproof** : 防水
2. **HMS** : 陛下的船

The *HMS Challenger.*

Oceanography today

Today oceanography is particularly important because petroleum and natural gas are often found on the ocean floor and oil platforms [1] are used to extract [2] them. Oceanography also helps us understand global climate changes. The Earth's atmosphere, its weather and its oceans are closely connected.

In 1929 the Americans Edward Beebe and Otis Barton invented the steel bathysphere with a window. It did not have a motor and was lowered deep into the sea with a long cable [3] . In 1934 the two men set a world record of 3,028 feet underwater. They sat in the sphere and were fascinated by the wonderful sea life they saw around them.

Barton and Beebe stand beside their invention, the bathysphere (1932).

The Swiss scientist and explorer Auguste Piccard invented the first bathyscaphe in 1947. The bathyscaphe, like the bathysphere, was an underwater vessel that was taken to its area of operation by a ship or a large submarine. But, unlike the bathysphere, the bathyscaphe had its own motor and could move by itself. In 1957 Piccard built an

1. **an oil platform** : 石油平台

2. **extract** : 提煉

3. **cable** : 鐵纜

improved bathyscaphe, called *Trieste*, which he later sold to the United States Navy.

In 1960 the *Trieste* went to the bottom of the Mariana Trench, the deepest part of the Earth's oceans, with a crew of two men: Piccard's son, Jacques, and Donald Walsh, a United States Navy Officer. It took the two men almost five hours to reach 32,808 feet in depth. They stayed on the ocean floor about twenty minutes and then spent more than three hours going up to the surface [1]. The *Trieste* had a very strong electric light and the men were able to see small, flat fish swimming around in the deep, dark trench. Piccard and Wash were the first men to explore the Mariana Trench. Today the deepest part of the Mariana Trench is called Challenger Deep, in honour of the *HMS Challenger*. The Challenger Deep is more than 7,000 feet (more than two kilometres) deeper than Mount Everest is high!

1.   **surface** : 表面

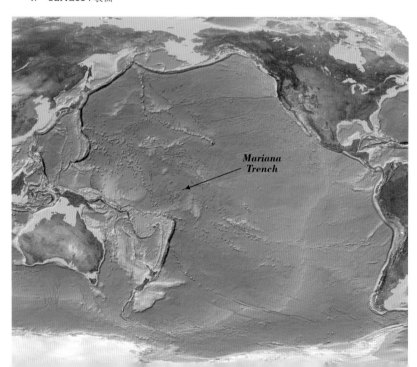

Mariana Trench

In 1995 the Japanese robotic submarine [1] *Kaiko* went down 35,797 feet into the Challenger Deep, and collected material from the trench.

In May 2009 the California Academy of Sciences and Hawkes Ocean Technology introduced *Deep Flight Super Falcon,* a new kind of submarine called a submersible. It is a manned [2], winged submarine that can fly underwater at high speeds and will be used for exploring the oceans of the world.

On 31 May 2009 another robotic submarine called *Nereus* reached the Challenger Deep at 35,769 feet. The *Nereus* was built by the Woods Hole Oceanographic Institution in Massachusetts, USA. The project manager of the *Nereus* said, 'With a robot like *Nereus* we can now explore anywhere in the ocean'.

The final frontier: space

Space is the final frontier; it is the explorer's last goal. The first space flight took place in October 1957 with a Russian satellite called *Sputnik 1*, which circled the Earth for three months. *Sputnik 1* surprised the entire world. After only three months, in January 1958, the United States sent its first satellite, *Explorer 1*, into space. This was the beginning of the space age and the space race between Russia and the United States.

Sputnik model (1957).

1. **robotic submarine**：機械人潛水艇
2. **manned**：載人

Buzz Aldrin on the Moon (1969).

On 12 April 1961 Russian astronaut Yuri Gagarin became the first person to travel in space. He travelled at the speed of 17,026 miles an hour and his flight lasted 108 minutes.

On 20 July 1969 television audiences all over the world watched two American astronauts walk on the Moon's surface! Astronaut Neil Armstrong was the first person to walk on the Moon, followed by Buzz Aldrin. They spent a day on the Moon before returning to Earth. This was a great achievement. Between 1969 and 1972 there were six other American manned moon landings.

The United States and Russia have built huge permanent space stations where astronauts can live, work and do scientific experiments. *Skylab* was the first space station launched [1] by NASA, the United States Space Agency, in 1973; it remained in space until 1979.

NASA also launched a reusable [2] spacecraft called the Space Shuttle in 1979, for human space missions. However the Shuttle is very expensive to operate and has had many problems. It will stop flying in 2010.

Space stations, space probes and more

In 1998 several countries — the United States, Russia, Europe, Japan, Canada, China and Brazil — decided to build the International Space Station, which was completed by 2011. It will be the largest space station to circle the earth and will travel at

1. **launched** : 發射
2. **reusable** : 可回收

the speed of 17,227 miles an hour, circling the Earth fifteen times a day. The main purpose of this station is scientific research in the fields of biology, astronomy and physics.

Space probes are another way of exploring space. They are unmanned robotic spacecrafts that explore our solar system. In November 1971 *Mariner 9* was the first space probe to travel to the planet Mars and circle it. It took more than seven thousand pictures of Mars's surface and scientists learned a lot about this planet. The pictures showed dust storms, ice clouds, morning fog, ancient river beds and volcanoes. It stopped working in October 1972.

The Mars Exploration Rovers [1] , *Spirit* and *Opportunity,* landed on Mars in 2004, and explored its surface and studied its soil and rocks. The University of Arizona in the United States was the first public university to take part in NASA's 'Scout Program': The Phoenix Mars Mission. In August 2007 NASA sent a small spacecraft called a lander to study the surface of Mars. The results of the mission were surprising.

1.   **a rover :**

Professor Peter Smith of the University of Arizona, Tucson, said that minerals, chemicals and water ice were found, which meant that there was a wetter and warmer climate on Mars millions of years ago.

Voyager 2, another American probe, was launched in 1977 and visited the planets Jupiter and Saturn, sending us pictures of their moons. *Voyager 2* is so far from Earth that it will never return. These space probes are extraordinary instruments that help us explore and understand our Solar System and beyond.

FACT FILE 知識檔案

NASA's Astrobiology Program

For centuries people have asked themselves if there is any form of life beyond the earth. People have talked about aliens, Martians and UFOs [1], and there are many films, books and websites on the subject. But no one has found an answer yet. However, NASA is trying to answer this important question with its Astrobiology Program.

Astrobiology is the study of the origin, evolution and future of life in the universe. NASA's programme started in 1996 and wants to answer these three questions:

- How does life begin and evolve?
- Is there life beyond Earth?
- What is the future of life on Earth and in the universe?

Professor John Baross, an astrobiologist at NASA and oceanographer at the University of Washington, Seattle, U.S.A., recently said, 'Our investigation made clear that life is possible in forms different than those on Earth.' Does he have the answer?

---

1. **UFOs**：不明飛行物

The text and **beyond**

1 Comprehension check

Complete the sentences (1-12) with their endings (A-L).

1 ☐ The bottom of the ocean is

2 ☐ In 1690 Edmond Halley and other men dived to 60 feet

3 ☐ David Bushnell invented the first

4 ☐ There was a complete laboratory for scientific research

5 ☐ The *Trieste* reached

6 ☐ A submersible is

7 ☐ *Sputnik 1* was a Russian satellite

8 ☐ A Russian called Yuri Gagarin

9 ☐ The first men to walk on the moon's surface

10 ☐ The International Space Station

11 ☐ It will be able to

12 ☐ Space probes and rovers

A a new kind of submarine used for exploring the oceans.

B submarine in 1775 and called it *The Turtle*.

C on the British ship *HMS Challenger*.

D was the world's first astronaut.

E very dark and cold.

F collect scientific information in space.

G the deepest part of the Earth's ocean called the Mariana Trench.

H in a diving bell in the River Thames.

I that circled the Earth for the first time in 1957.

J is being built by different countries.

K are unmanned robotic spacecrafts for space exploration.

L were Neil Armstrong and Buzz Aldrin.

❷ Vocabulary

Find the words from Chapter Seven which are defined below.

1 can be used many times ....
2 with a person on board ....
3 the study of the solar system, the stars and outer space ....
4 the top of something ....
5 the study and exploration of the oceans ....
6 sent into space ....
7 the weight of something creates this ....
8 a long rope made of steel ....
9 a submarine that has no crew and is operated by people on a ship ....

PET ❸ Sentence transformation

Look at these sentences. For each question, complete the second sentence so that it means the same as the first, using no more than three words.

0 He had a waterproof diving suit on.
  He ..was wearing.. a waterproof diving suit.

1 The bathyscaphe was trying to find the deepest part of the ocean.
  The bathyscaphe .... the deepest part of the ocean.

2 The astronauts were worried when they heard the message from the scientist.
  The astronauts were worried when they heard .... said.

3 Details of the submersible are available from the engineer.
  You can .... of the submersible from the engineer.

4 Scientists continue referring to the *HMS Challenger*.
  Scientists have not .... to the *HMS Challenger*.

4 Discussion

The exploration of space is a very expensive operation. A huge amount is spent on space programmes every year. Some people say that this money could be spent in better ways. How do you feel about this? Divide the class into two groups and prepare a debate. One team can defend the space operations and the other team can be against them. What is the result? Give good reasons for your opinions.

5 Writing

You are an astronaut in a new Space Station. Write in your diary about 35-45 words to say:

- how it feels to be in a Space Station
- how things are different from your life on Earth
- what scientific material you are looking for.

INTERNET PROJECT

Let's explore Mars!

There are several space programmes for the exploration of Mars. Divide the class into three groups. Each group can discuss:

- overview
- science
- all about Mars.

Then the whole class can enjoy the videos from Mars on Multimedia.

1 Discussing pictures

Look at the pictures below. They all come from different chapters in this book. Work with a partner. Describe what you can see in each picture and what you have learnt about it.

2 Crossword puzzle

Across

2 They kept food from going bad.

3 Disease caused by lack of vitamin C.

4 They sailed in longships.

7 First person to walk on Moon.

10 United States space agency.

11 Cook called them the Sandwich Islands.

12 Great explorer of Africa.

Down

1 Study and exploration of oceans.

3 Manned winged submarine.

5 She helped Lewis and Clark.

6 He was killed in the Philippines.

8 He explored the South Pacific.

9 Norwegian explorer.

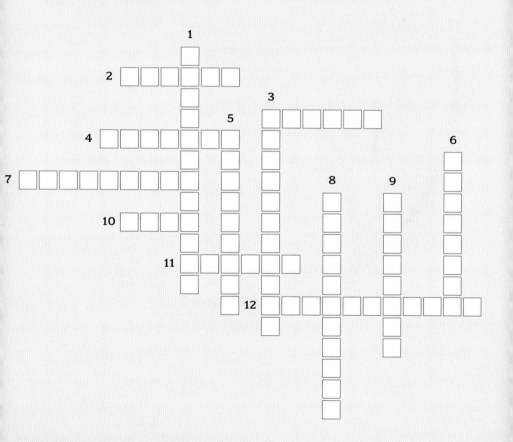

Black Cat Discovery 閱讀系列：

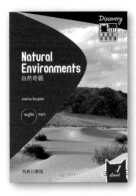

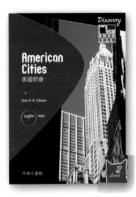

Level 1 and 2